Dear Parent:
Your child's love of reading starts here!

I Can Read Books have introduced children to the joy of reading since 1957. Featuring award-winning authors and illustrators and a fabulous cast of beloved characters, I Can Read Books set the standard for beginning readers. From books your child reads with you to the first books they read alone, there are I Can Read Books for every stage of reading:

SHARED READING
Basic language, word repetition, and whimsical illustrations, ideal for sharing with your emergent reader

BEGINNING READING
Short sentences, familiar words, and simple concepts for children eager to read on their own

READING WITH HELP
Engaging stories, longer sentences, and language play for developing readers

READING ALONE
Complex plots, challenging vocabulary, and high-interest topics for the independent reader

ADVANCED READING
Short paragraphs, chapters, and exciting themes for the perfect bridge to chapter books

Every child learns in a different way and at their own speed. Some read through each level in order. Others go back and forth between levels and read favorite books again and again. You can help your young reader improve and become more confident by encouraging their own interests and abilities.

A lifetime of discovery begins with the magical words, "I Can Read!"

For Teryl Hodgdon, for all her kindness
—E.H.M.

For Kelly, Niffles, and Moo
—B.L.

HarperCollins®, ☙®, and I Can Read Book® are trademarks of HarperCollins Publishers Inc.

Library of Congress Cataloging-in-Publication Data
Minarik, Else Holmelund.
  Cat and dog / by Else Holmelund Minarik ; pictures by Bryan Langdo.
    p.   cm. — (My first I can read book)
  Summary: A young child monitors a cat and dog as they romp through the house and garden.
  ISBN 0-06-074247-X — ISBN 0-06-074248-8 (lib. bdg.)
  [1. Cats—Fiction. 2. Dogs—Fiction.] I. Langdo, Bryan, ill. II. Title. III. Series.
PZ7.M652Cat 2005   2004022474
[E]—dc22   CIP
                                                                                                                      AC

1 2 3 4 5 6 7 8 9 10   ❖   First Edition

MY FIRST
I Can Read Book®

CAT AND DOG

BY THE AUTHOR OF *LITTLE BEAR*
ELSE HOLMELUND MINARIK
PICTURES BY BRYAN LANGDO

HarperCollins*Publishers*

Off the bed,

Cat, Cat,

Or I'll make

A catball out of you,

I will, I will."

"Meow, meow,
I'll get off,
I will, I will."

"Woof! Woof!
Off the chair,
Cat, Cat,

Or I'll make
A catcoat out of you,
I will, I will."

"Meow, meow,
I'll get off,
I will, I will."

"Woof! Woof!
Off the table,
Cat, Cat,

Or I'll make
A catpie out of you,
I will, I will."

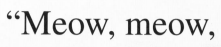

"Meow, meow,

Come and get me,
Dog, Dog,
If you can,
If you can."

"Here! Here!
Off the table,
Silly Dog,
Silly Cat.

Animals on the table!
My goodness!
The very idea."

"Meow—Meow—

Out of the water,
Dog, Dog.
You will make the house wet,
You will, you will."

"Woof! Woof!
Here I come.
Here I come."

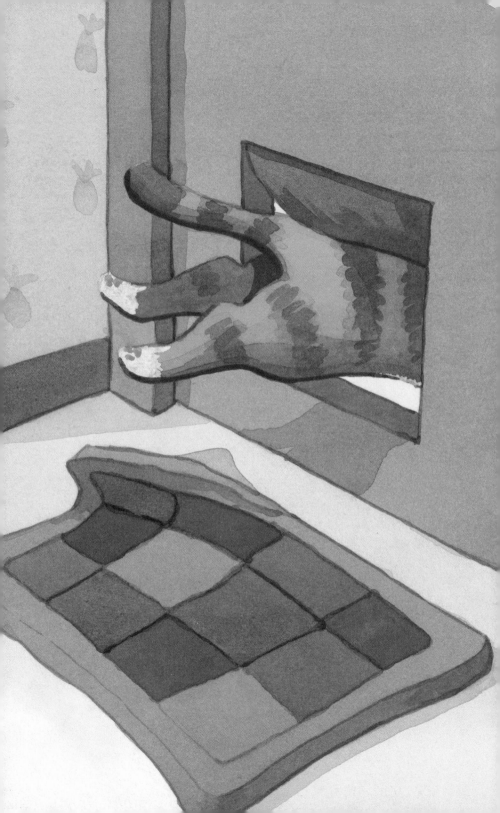

"Meow—Meow—

Out of the garden,
Dog, Dog.
You will be tied up—
You will, you will."

"Woof! Woof!
Here I come.
I am coming."

"Meow—Meow—
Here are bones,
Dog, Dog.

Get them out.

Get them out."

"Woof! Woof!
Bones for me
—and for you.
Bones for us."

"Here! Here!
Silly Cat.
Silly Dog.
What is this?

Are you so hungry?

Well, then,

I will feed you."

"Are you happy now?
Good."